Maggie and Me

Maggie and Me

TED STAUNTON

VIKING

Kids Can Press Ltd. acknowledges with appreciation
the assistance of the Canada Council
and the Ontario Arts Council
in the production of this book.

VIKING
Published by the Penguin Group
Viking Penguin, a division of Penguin Books USA Inc.,
40 West 23rd Street, New York, New York 10010, U.S.A.
Penguin Books Ltd, 27 Wrights Lane, London W8 5TZ, England
Penguin Books Australia Ltd, Ringwood, Victoria, Australia
Penguin Books Canada Ltd, 2801 John Street, Markham, Ontario, Canada L3R 1B4
Penguin Books (N.Z.) Ltd, 182–190 Wairau Road, Auckland 10, New Zealand

Penguin Books Ltd, Registered Offices: Harmondsworth, Middlesex, England

First published in Canada by Kids Can Press Ltd., 1986
First American edition published 1990
1 3 5 7 9 10 8 6 4 2
Copyright © Ted Staunton, 1986
All rights reserved

Inspiration for the experiments in "Thunder and Lightning" came from *Scienceworks*, an
Ontario Science Centre Book of Experiments, published by Kids Can Press Ltd.

LIBRARY OF CONGRESS CATALOGING IN PUBLICATION DATA
Staunton, Ted, 1956–
Maggie and me / Ted Staunton.—1st American ed.
p.   cm.—(The Greenapple Street geniuses)
Reprint. Originally published: Toronto : Kids Can Press, 1986.
Summary: Cyril may be small for his age, but he does not worry
about bullies because of his partnership with Maggie, the "Genius of
Greenapple Street."
ISBN 0-670-83169-7   [1. Friendship—Fiction.]   I. Title.   II. Series.
PZ7.S8076Mag   1990   [E]—dc20   89-22574

Printed in the United States of America.
Set in Century Book.

For Mike and Friends

Contents

Maggie and Me

Best Dressed Bully

For a long time that Sunday afternoon, I couldn't figure it out. Somehow Maggie looked different. Then, as we were walking up Greenapple Street, it hit me.

"Hey," I said, "You're wearing a dress."

"Brilliant, Cyril," she snapped. "Maybe you should be the genius around here." Everybody knew that the Greenapple Street genius was Maggie.

"How come you're wearing a dress?" I asked.

"Because I have to. We're going to my Grandma's."

"So what's wrong with wearing a dress?" I asked.

"Everything!" moaned Maggie. "I can't have any fun. I have to stay neat all the time. I have to keep pulling my socks up. You can't climb trees in a dress. You can't build forts. You can't have crabapple wars. You have to wear an apron just to use a chemistry set. You can't ride a bike..."

"You can too ride a bike," I said. I didn't know, but I didn't see why not, and I wanted to say something.

Maggie looked at me. "Bet?" she asked.

"Bet," I said, but I should have known better.

"Come with me," said Maggie, as she led me towards her garage. All of a sudden, she seemed a lot more cheerful.

The next thing I knew, Maggie had me wearing an old dress her Mom was going to get rid of.

"No fair," I said. "This thing is way too long."

"Yes fair," said Maggie. "You just said a dress. You never said what kind. Now, get on my bike. If you can ride to the schoolyard and back, you're boss for a week. If you can't, I am."

I climbed on her bike and started down Green-apple Street. It was like riding in a tent. The dress was everywhere, flapping around and whirring when it slapped the spokes. I couldn't see my feet. I couldn't even see my hands.

I wobbled into the schoolyard and began to turn around. Suddenly everything stopped moving. There was a tearing sound and I landed on the ground, all tangled up in pedals and spokes and dress.

"Bwaa! Help!" I yelled. It felt like I was drowning in cloth.

There were footsteps, then a voice I knew.

"Hey, look who's here," the voice said. It sounded pleased.

When I pulled the dress away from my face, I was looking up at Ugly Augie Crumley and his Goons, the biggest bullies in school. I shuddered.

"Nice dress, Cyril," said Ugly Augie. The Goons all giggled.

"Doesn't Cyril look cute, you guys?" The Goons giggled some more.

"Gee, Cyril, did your Mommy get you all *dressed* up?" I thought the Goons were going to die laughing. My face got very red.

"What are we going to do to him, Augie?" asked one of the Goons. They were still scared to touch me since the time I gave them all poison ivy with a bag of pennies.

"Nothing," said Ugly Augie, "except tell everybody about how Cyril wears dresses. C'mon, you guys. See you at school tomorrow, Cyril. Wear something nice."

They went off laughing and yelling and pretending they were carrying purses. I sat there and sighed. It looked like I was going to get picked on all over again.

By the time I got untangled and went back up Greenapple Street, Maggie had already gone to her Grandma's. She left a note on her garage door. "You Lose The Bet," it said. I had to be miserable by myself until Monday.

On Monday morning, I told Maggie what happened.

"Everybody will laugh at me," I complained.

"We'll see," said Maggie. Then, because she was boss, she made me carry a big book she was reading about knights and dragons.

I was right. Everybody laughed. And whispered. They pointed at me too. Ugly Augie and the Goons kept asking where my dress was. I tried to explain, but nobody wanted to listen.

All day long it got worse until I wanted to run away and hide somewhere.

By lunch time, I felt sick.

Maggie said "Cyril, I think we might have to take care of Crumley all over again."

"But I don't know what to do!" I wailed.

"Leave it to me," said Maggie. "This is just the kind of problem I like. I haven't had a good problem in a long time."

Then she went off with her book about knights and queens and stuff and I went to find a place to hide. It took a while. I'd just found a good place in some bushes when something amazing happened.

Maggie came marching across the schoolyard, carrying her book and a baseball glove. She went right up to Crumley, opened the book, and called out so everyone could hear, "Ugly Augie Crumley, you are challenged to a duel by Cyril of Greenapple. You have spoken many lies and bad things about him all day. Tomorrow after school, you must answer for them here. Cyril of Greenapple will pick the weapons and rules of the duel

10

because his honour has been challenged.''

Everybody gasped, especially me.

Maggie looked down at her book. "Oh yeah," she said. "If you are not a snivelling coward, you will pick up the glove I throw at your feet to accept this challenge.''

She threw the baseball glove on Ugly Augie's foot.

"Yoww," he cried. A rock fell out of the glove. He looked at the glove. Everybody looked at Ugly Augie.

"What's the matter, Crumley?'' said Maggie. "Chicken?''

Ugly Augie grabbed the glove. Maggie snatched it back.

"After school tomorrow," she said and ran away.

As we walked home from school, Maggie was pleased with herself.

"That was perfect," she chuckled, "especially the rock.''

"What do you mean perfect?'' I yelled at her. "Ugly Augie will kill me!''

"Not if I make up the right rules," said Maggie. "And just remember our bet. I'm boss, so you do what I say.''

"Aw," I groaned. Sometimes doing what Maggie said could get you in even worse trouble than you were in already.

"I just hope I have time to think of something,''

11

said Maggie. "I promised my Dad I'd do some baking with him tonight." She took her book from me and went up the driveway to her house.

"You mean you don't know the rules yet?" I called after her, but she was already inside. I went home feeling even more miserable than before.

All day Tuesday, everybody talked about the duel —everybody except Maggie, who walked around acting mysterious, and me. I was too scared to talk. I wasn't sure that this was any better than being laughed at.

Every so often Ugly Augie would talk about using me for a broom, and I'd get a prickly feeling up my back. I still didn't know what the rules were.

After lunch, Maggie brought a big bag to school. When she wasn't looking, I peeked inside. There was a cloth, two buckets, two strainers like the ones we had in the kitchen, and a box of Flako Shortening. She must still be baking, I thought. I wish she'd start thinking about the duel.

I decided to sneak away after school. But I couldn't. After school, every kid in the whole class was waiting by the doors.

"What are you going to do, Cyril?" they all started asking. I was trapped.

"You'll see," I said. Before I could get away, they marched me right into the schoolyard.

Across the field came Ugly Augie and the Goons.

"Let's get started," snarled Ugly Augie. The Goons were all slapping hands.

I looked around. Where was Maggie? I didn't know what to do. My legs felt like they were turning to mush.

Then everyone stood aside and Maggie bustled up with two buckets of water. She put the buckets five steps apart.

"Hear ye, hear ye," yelled Maggie. "The duel is about to begin. Duellers, to your buckets."

She pointed. Crumley and I each stood beside a bucket.

"The duel is a water fight," Maggie announced. "These are your weapons." She took the two strainers out of her back pockets. The crowd began to buzz.

"That's stupid," said Ugly Augie. "The water will run right through them."

"That's what makes it hard," said Maggie. "Duels aren't supposed to be easy. Whoever gets the other person wetter in two minutes wins. No moving feet allowed. And the loser has to stay dressed up for a week." There was a gasp from the crowd.

"Now I'll wipe off the weapons," said Maggie. "They have to be perfectly clean and dry."

Out came the cloth. She wiped Ugly Augie's strainer with one side and mine with the other. Then she gave them to us. Ugly Augie swatted the air with his strainer. My teeth chattered.

"All right," said Maggie. "Stand up straight and hold your weapon over your heart. When I

13

say go, you start throwing. And may the best kid win.''

She looked at her watch. Everything went very quiet.

"Ready," she said. "Set. Go!!"

Everyone yelled, and Ugly Augie went wild. He was throwing water like he had ten arms. I was so frightened that I couldn't move at all. I closed my eyes and waited for the water to hit me.

But, except for a few drops on my nose, I didn't feel anything. I opened my eyes. The crowd was jumping up and down. Ugly Augie was still throwing. The grass around him was all wet.

"Come on, Cyril," yelled Maggie. "Come on!"

More people started to yell for me, and slowly I began to move.

I dipped the strainer in the water, lifted it, and threw. A big scoop of water smacked Ugly Augie right in the face. The crowd screamed. I stared. He stared. I looked at the strainer. It looked okay to me.

"Thirty seconds," cried Maggie.

I tried it again. This time I soaked his stomach. The crowd roared. Now it was my turn to throw like crazy. Ugly Augie ducked and dodged, but he still got soaked.

"Time's up!" called Maggie. The crowd was stomping and cheering.

"No fair," screeched Ugly Augie and grabbed

his bucket. It still had lots of water in it. He took one step toward me and slipped on the wet grass. The bucket flew up, and water drenched the Goons who were standing behind him.

"Cyril wins! Cyril wins!" everybody yelled.

"Make sure you're dressed up tomorrow, Crumley," said Maggie, "or everyone will be making fun of you. Let's go, Cyril of Greenapple." She handed me all the equipment and we headed for home.

I was feeling pretty proud of myself.

"Gee," I said, "I didn't know I had such good aim. It was just like magic."

Maggie laughed. "It was just like baking, Cyril."

"What?" I asked.

"My Dad showed me last night," said Maggie. "If you wipe shortening all over a strainer, it holds water just like a bucket and it's hard to see. So I thought of a water fight and your duel. Today, when I wiped off the strainers, I had shortening on one side of that cloth—the side that wiped your strainer. I set it up so you couldn't lose. Which is why I'm the Greenapple Street genius."

"Oh," I said. I liked it better when I was the hero. Still, it was nice to know that Maggie didn't let me down.

"Thanks," I said.

"Don't mention it," said Maggie. "I think this afternoon you should wash my bike."

On Wednesday, Ugly Augie came to school all dressed up. I practically didn't recognize him. I had never seen him with a tie and combed hair before. Neither had anyone else, but we were all scared to tease him, except the Goons. They asked him who he had a big date with and when was he getting married and were all the girls in love with him.

Ugly Augie couldn't play with anybody, because he wasn't allowed to get his good clothes all messed up. After a while, I felt a little sorry for him.

Then something strange happened. On Thursday, the Goons came to school all dressed up. Their parents thought Ugly Augie looked so nice that they made the Goons wear their good clothes too.

By Friday, we were all dressed up. Everybody's parents had decided they wanted us to look just like Crumley and the Goons.

Now nobody could play and get dirty. We all stood around staring at each other and waiting for the bell to ring. My good shoes hurt my feet. Even worse, everybody blamed me for starting it.

"Maggie made the rules," I said. Nobody listened.

At lunch it rained. Nobody was allowed to get wet. When it stopped, we all gathered around a big mud puddle in the middle of the schoolyard and stared at it.

Then I got my idea—the best idea of my life. For a minute, I held it inside and kept it secret. It was so nice. When I couldn't keep it in any longer, I started to smile.

I looked at Maggie and made a sign. She smiled and nodded. She was thinking the same thing. Very slowly, very quietly, we stepped back from everybody. We put up our hands, counted to three, and pushed two Goons as hard as we could. They bumped into three kids, who bounced off four more, who knocked Ugly Augie right into the mud.

"Hey!" he yelled and dragged them in after him.

"Hey!!" they yelled and grabbed the people that pushed them.

I didn't even wait. I jumped right in. In a few seconds, everyone was dirty and yelling, laughing and having a great time. It felt nice to be dirty even if our good clothes did get wrecked.

Everybody got in trouble, especially me, because I started it. But it was all worth it because it meant not having to dress up for school anymore.

Everyone thanked me. "It was Maggie's idea, too," I said.

"You thought of it first, Cyril," said Maggie. "It was a great idea, and I should know because I thought of it too." She shook my hand.

"Maybe we should be partners," she said.

"Fantastic," I said.

17

"Of course," said Maggie. "you'll have to do everything I say."

Thunder and Lightning

"Some things go together, even though they're not the same," said Mr. Flynn, our teacher in Room 7. "There's thunder and lightning, shoes and socks. Can anybody think of others?"

"Bread and butter," said Monica Goodman.

"Sure," said Mr. Flynn.

"Milk and cereal," said Lester.

"Hats and heads," called somebody else from the back of the room.

"Boys and girls," said Bobby Devlin. Everybody giggled.

"Mountains and valleys," said my friend Maggie, the Greenapple Street genius.

"That's interesting," said Mr. Flynn. "Why do mountains and valleys go together, Maggie?"

"If you didn't have something low with something high or something high with something low, you'd never know that one was high and the other was low."

"I never thought of it like that," said Mr. Flynn. "Sometimes you need mountains to know you have valleys." He twirled his big brown moustache.

Bobby Devlin shuffled in his chair.

"All these things work together even though they're different," said Mr. Flynn. "And we're going to think about that for the next little while. We're going to pick partners and do science projects to discover how three things on earth work together—land, water, and air."

I looked at Maggie. She looked at me and nodded. We were partners again.

"Just to get you warmed up," said Mr. Flynn, "I'm going to give you some homework." Everybody groaned.

"Pick a partner, if you want to, and see if you can solve three science puzzles. You won't get the answers by just thinking about them. You'll have to experiment." Then Mr. Flynn wrote three questions on the blackboard:

How can you throw a ball away from you and make it come back without bouncing?
How can you drop a coin on a table and make it stay on edge for three seconds?
How can you make a lump of modeling clay float?

"See if you can find some answers for tomorrow," said Mr. Flynn. He was twirling his moustache so that it curled up even higher than usual.

"Which one will we do first?" I asked Maggie as we walked home along Greenapple Street.

"Number one, of course," she said, "but I'm doing these by myself."

"Aren't we partners?" I asked.

"We're partners for the project, but I think better alone. That's the kind of genius I am."

"Then how will we do our project?" I asked.

"I'll do the thinking and you'll do the doing. Just do everything I say."

"That's not being partners," I said, "That's you being boss. I can think too, you know."

"Okay," said Maggie, "You think you're so smart. Let's bet. If you can answer any one of these questions before I can, I won't be boss."

I thought about the last time I bet with Maggie. I got caught wearing a dress by Ugly Augie Crumley and I had to fight a duel. It was awful. But this bet looked easy. I only had to get one question first—one question and Maggie wouldn't be boss. I got pretty tired of Maggie being boss sometimes.

"Okay," I said.

"Starting right now," Maggie yelled. She began to run and I took off right behind her.

I got to my room and opened my notebook to

the first question, *How can you throw a ball away from you and make it come back without bouncing?*

"Easy," I said, as I grabbed my best tennis ball and headed outside.

How could I make it come back without bouncing? I threw it down and it jumped up. That was no good. I threw it at the garage door and it bounced back at me. I tossed it behind me but it hit the house and came back. I threw it down the street and it didn't come back at all. When I finally found it, I put a spin on it and let it go behind my back. It hit the car next door and bounced into a prickle bush. I got all scratched pulling it out, and the man next door stared at me from his window.

Mr. Flynn's question was harder than it looked. What was left to do? I stood in the driveway tossing the ball up to my nose and catching it while I thought. Then I saw what I was doing. I was so surprised I threw the ball a little too high and it landed on my head. That was it! The ball came back.

I raced to Maggie's yelling, "I got it. I got it! What you do is..."

"Throw the ball straight up," said Maggie, without looking up from her work table. "I got it ages ago. I'm already on number two."

"Oh," I said.

I ran back home and read the second question,

How can you drop a coin on a table and make it stay on edge for three seconds?

My piggy bank was open in a second. Coins dropped like rain, but they didn't stay on their edges. I got a little worried. When I tried again to make a coin stand up by itself, it wouldn't work until I rolled it. Then it rolled right off the table.

At last I figured it out. To make the coin stand up, you had to spin it before it hit the table. Figuring it out was easier than doing it. My fingers felt like spaghetti. Finally, I held the coin with my thumb at the bottom and my first finger at the top. Then I flicked it with my second finger as I let go. It bounced and spun and stayed spinning for three seconds. I was out the door before it stopped.

"Wait. Hold everything!" I yelled as loud as I could. "You can keep the coin up if you..."

"Spin it as you drop it," said Maggie. "Are you still on that one?"

I couldn't believe it. How could Maggie be so fast? I was down to my last chance.

"I'm looking for some modelling clay," said Maggie, as she burrowed through a box of junk. "Have you got any?"

I was so mad. I almost said no, even though I had some, but then I said, "yeah."

"Never mind," she said, "I found some."

I headed for home fast.

As the sink filled with water, I bit my nails.

23

Every second I thought I heard Maggie yelling, "I've got it!"

No matter what I did, the clay wouldn't float —in cold water, hot water, or just plain water. The more times it sank, the madder I got, until finally I grabbed it out of the sink in a big lump and threw it on the bathroom floor.

"Stupid junk," I said and stomped on it.

The clay squished flat under my foot and stuck to the bottom of my running shoe. I peeled it off and threw it in the sink. It floated—just like a raft.

I flew down the stairs.

"Maaaaaaaaaaaaaaaa- gggiieeeeeeeeee! Times! Times! I've got it!" Maggie watched me come up the driveway. At her feet was a bucket. Inside it, a flat piece of modelling clay was floating.

"Beat you Cyril," she said. "I win the bet. Too bad. Not everybody can be a genius."

"I almost beat you," I said.

"Did not," said Maggie. "You weren't even close. I thought I was going to be 90 years old waiting for you. But if you do what I say from now on, we can be partners like before."

All of a sudden, I was very angry.

"No," I said. "You think you're so smart, always bossing me around. I don't want to do my science project with you anymore."

"Good," said Maggie. "I don't want to do mine with you either. I don't even want to play with a sore loser like you."

The next morning, I told Mr. Flynn I wanted to do my project alone. "I think better by myself," I said. "Besides, I'm tired of partners. They always boss you around and make you do stuff their way."

"Partners are supposed to share, not boss," said Mr. Flynn. "Try it on your own Cyril, but tell me if you change your mind."

Mr. Flynn split the class into three groups, one for the land, one for the air, and one for the water. He gave us a lot of questions. We were supposed to pick one and go to the library to look up a science experiment that would help us answer it. Then we had to do the experiment, write a report, and bring it all in on the same day to show everybody. It was going to be like a science fair. The principal would come and look at everybody's work.

"When you've all finished working together," said Mr. Flynn, "we'll see what the projects show us about how the land, wind, and water work together."

Maggie and I were both put in the water group. Right away I started planning how I was going to do better than she would. The first thing I had to do was beat her to the best books in the school library.

After school, I was first to the closet to get my jacket. There was just one problem. Someone had tied it up in knots with five others. While I tugged and struggled, Maggie took her own jacket from her desk and raced out the door.

By the time I got to the library, Maggie had the best books.

"Now I'm going to the public library," I heard her tell the librarian. The public library! Why hadn't I thought of that?

I hurried outside, behind again. And then I saw my chance. Maggie was kneeling by her bike, tying her shoe. Before she knew what was happening, I ran up, leaped on her bike, and took off for home.

"See you at the library," I called.

"Cyril, you jerk!" she shouted.

I left the bike at Maggie's and ran to my house. "Mom," I called, "Can we go to the library right now?"

Maggie was panting up the street as we drove off.

This time I got the best books. We were just driving away from the public library when Maggie got there. It was all even again.

That night I got down to work. I picked the question, *Where does rain come from?* My Dad and I looked through all the experiments in the books and picked the best one.

"Let's try it," my Dad said.

We got a pink plastic tub from the basement.

"You used to have your baths in that when you were a baby," said my mother.

"Oh Mom," I said. I hated that kind of stuff.

Next, we got some dirt from the garden. We dumped it in the tub, put in lots of water, and swirled it around until we had a big muddy puddle, just like the book said.

We borrowed a glass from the kitchen and tried to stand it up in the middle of the puddle. The glass kept tipping over and floating, so I read the book again. It said to put a clean rock in the glass to make it heavy, so I went outside and got some stones. Then I washed them off and put them in the glass. With the stones in the bottom, the glass stood up.

My Dad and I stretched plastic wrap over the top of the tub and sealed it tight. At last I took another stone and put it on top of the plastic—right above the glass.

"Now what?" asked my Dad.

"The book says it has to sit in the sun all day," I said.

Dad wanted to take it outside and leave it there till morning, so we carried the tub to the backyard.

"It's supposed to rain in the tub," I told my

Dad. "How can it rain if it's all sealed up?"

"We'll see tomorrow," said Dad.

As we turned to go inside, I looked down the street. A yellow light shone in Maggie's garage. Through the open door I saw huge shadows dancing on the wall. For a second I got scared. What if she was doing something really fantastic?

"C'mon, Rainmaker," said my Dad. I followed him in. Rainmaker—that's what I'd call my project, I thought.

The next morning was sunny. I rushed outside to see if it had rained in the tub yet. The muddy puddle lay in the bottom. Nothing had changed. I'd have to wait till after school.

When I got home from school, I went straight to the Rainmaker. All I could see was a mist on the inside of the plastic wrap and some drops of water that had gathered below the large stone. Nothing moved, nothing rained.

Then I heard a plip. I bent down and peeked under the edge where the wrap wasn't misty. Plink. A clear drop of water fell from the wrap into the glass. It wasn't muddy, so maybe it was rain. But two or three drops aren't exactly a rainstorm, are they? The Rainmaker was not very exciting to look at. Something had to be wrong. I went inside and got the book.

But the book said everything was right. The sun warmed the water in the mud puddle and it "evaporated." It turned into something invisible called water vapour and rose through the air. That made the puddle get smaller, like puddles on the street when they dry up. As soon as the water vapour hit the plastic wrap, it turned back into little drops of water because the plastic was cooler than the air.

If my Dad and I hadn't put on the plastic wrap, the water vapour would have sailed high into the sky until it hit cold air. Then it would have turned back to water drops and become part of a cloud. I had a little cloud on the inside of my plastic wrap that was raining in my Rainmaker—but slowly and not very much.

I started to feel better. It was hard to see, but it was raining and it was my project. Maggie couldn't make it any better, I thought. Then I went outside to watch it rain some more.

As I got to the backyard, the sound of hammering floated down Greenapple Street. Maggie was standing on a ladder hammering something over her garage door. She was wearing a long white scientist's coat.

I had to see what she was doing, so I snuck down the street to the side of the garage. There were signs all over the place.

QUIET!
GENIUS WORKING!!

TOP SECRET!!!
DO NOT ENTER!!!

THIS LAB
PROTECTED BY
DEATH RAY!!!!!!!

Carefully, I peeked around the corner. Maggie had her back to me as she stood on the ladder. Inside the garage on a big table sat a kettle, a jug of water, a big spoon, a tray of ice cubes, a steel-girder building set, Christmas lights, library books, a flower pot, a doll with a toy umbrella, felt pens, and a box. A poster of the planets was stuck on the wall, and a rocket model hung from the ceiling.

"Get lost, Cyril," said a voice above me.

I froze.

"Can't you read?" Maggie dropped the sign she had been hammering over the doorway. It fell right in front of my nose. In red letters, it said KEEP OUT!!!!! There was a skull and crossbones underneath.

I went home feeling worried. Anything *that* secret had to be good, whatever it was. I looked at my Rainmaker again. Another drop plonked into the glass. Now it really looked dull.

My Mom and Dad thought the Rainmaker was

great, but I started to think it was no good. It just wasn't neat enough.

The next day I told Mr. Flynn that my project worked, but it looked dumb.

"That's okay," he said. "Lots of things in nature don't look amazing at first. What's amazing are their secrets. Rain is one secret of a river or a lake or a mud puddle, and you've found it out."

"Oh," I said.

"If you want to make your project better, Cyril, write a report about how you found the secret. Maybe draw a picture of how water changes into clouds and rain all around us. Then everybody can see how it works."

My report ended up being three pages long. I drew a big picture of how it rains. That made me feel a little better, until I went out to play and saw Maggie bustling around with boxes and pails of water.

I went back inside and made a big sign for my project that said THE RAINMAKER–SECRET OF A MUD PUDDLE. Then I painted grass and trees on the outside of the tub so my puddle would look more real.

On the morning we had to take our projects to school, I put everything in my wagon and pulled it down Greenapple Street. As I went along slowly, I heard a rolling noise coming from behind.

Then Maggie bustled past me, pulling her wagon, which was stacked with boxes.

"First one there gets the best spot," she yelled as she sped by. I couldn't go any faster without spilling the Rainmaker.

By the time I got to Room 7, Maggie was all set up. On one side of the desk in front of her, there was a kettle. Near the kettle was a tower she had built with her girder set. Sticking out from the tower was a big spoon. Underneath the spoon was a doll standing in a large flower pot and holding a little umbrella. At the back of the desk, there were ice cubes in a dish and a pair of tongs.

Maggie put on her white scientist's coat. With the tongs, she picked up two ice cubes and put them in the spoon. Then she plugged in the kettle. As the steam from the kettle hit the bottom of the cold spoon, it turned back into water and splattered down on the doll's umbrella. Maggie had made instant rain.

She stuck up a sign that said THE RAIN MACHINE. It had a little white light that flashed on and off.

I groaned and looked around. All over the classroom there were different science projects. If I could find a nice quiet corner, maybe no one would notice my dumb old Rainmaker. But the only place left was right beside Maggie.

Quietly I set up the Rainmaker on the table, hung up my picture and sign, and put out my report. Maggie stared, but I pretended I didn't see. I wondered when she would start to laugh and hung my head.

Kids that had finished setting up their projects started to come by.

"What's that, Cyril?" asked my friend Lester.

"It makes rain," I said.

"I don't see anything," said Monica.

I started to show them, but Lester said, "Oh wow! Look at that!" They turned to look at Maggie's Rain Machine.

After a minute, though, Monica said, "I don't get it. It doesn't really rain with kettles and ice cubes, does it?"

"*Real* rain gets made like this," I said and pointed at the Rainmaker.

"How?" said Lester. This time I showed them, and I told them all about it.

"Real rain takes a long time," I said. "And it's hard to see it getting made."

"Neat," said Monica.

"I like Maggie's," said Lester.

"This one's realer," said Monica.

"That one's neater," said Lester.

They were just starting to argue when Mr. Flynn walked in with the principal. Everything went quiet.

The principal was a big lady with white hair. She could smile like your grandma, but she was really strict when you got sent down to see her. Maggie and I had been down to see her a couple of times. But right now she was smiling.

They walked around the room. Mr. Flynn was twirling his moustache a lot. Nobody else moved except Maggie. She was doing something behind me, but I didn't dare turn around to see. I just wanted to melt into the floor.

At last they came to us.

"The Rain Machine and the Rainmaker," read the principal. She stared for a long time then said, "Don't these two go together well? I can see two ways of looking at the same problem. Here's the rain and there's how it's formed. Very good. All you two need is the thunder and lightning. Did you do your projects together?"

"No," I said.

"Yes," said Maggie.

I spun around. Maggie had stuck a piece of paper between our two signs. On it she had written the word AND with both of our names.

Maggie said quickly, "Cyril means that we did our own thinking and each made half. Then we put the halves together."

I started to get the idea.

"That way there was no bossing," I said.

"Good for you," said the principal.

Mr. Flynn twisted his moustache and didn't say anything. He just stared at us for a while.

As they moved away, I whispered to Maggie, "Do you want to be partners again?"

"We'd better be," she whispered back.

"My ideas and your ideas? No bossing?" I said, just to make sure.

Maggie thought for a minute. "Only bossing if you ask me to help you," she said.

"Okay," I said. We shook hands and were partners again.

"Yours is neat to watch," I said.   ·

"Yours is realer," said Maggie.

"We need thunder and lightning," I said.

"You can be the thunder," said Maggie, thumping the side of my tub. "I'll be the lightning." She pointed to the flashing light bulb. I felt better already.

"As long as we keep thinking up great ideas like these, we'll be fine," said Maggie.

I started to say that my idea came out of a library book, then I stopped. Maggie's probably had too. As long as there were enough library books for both of us, we'd probably be fine. Except...

"What will we tell Mr. Flynn?" I asked.

"Asking for help?" said Maggie. "Don't worry, just say what I say."

Hockey Stuck

It was the old glop trick. I fell for it every time. Chocolate glop was my favourite dessert—ice cream, chocolate sauce, and bananas all mushed together. We only had it after I'd been really good. Or before I had to do something I really didn't like. My Mom figured I'd be so happy about the glop, I wouldn't mind as much.

"It's time for Saturday classes at the community school again," Mom announced. "What do you want to take this fall, Cyril?"

"Nothing," I said, as fast as I could. Now I knew why I was having chocolate glop. I hated Saturday classes. Everybody but me always seemed to know everybody else. I was the only one who was never any good at what we were doing.

"You can meet new friends," said my Dad, "and learn something new. There's lots to choose from."

"I don't like doing any of that stuff," I said.

"You haven't heard what there is yet." My Dad read from the list in the booklet, "There's judo, crafts, floor hockey, baton, piano, and gymnastics."

"Yuck," I said.

"Cyril," said my Dad. He read the list again. Maybe there was one I liked after all.

"Piano," I said.

"You can't take that, dear," said my Mom. "We don't have a piano."

"How about floor hockey?" asked my Dad.

I knew what that meant—getting picked last, never getting a pass, getting pushed around by the big guys.

"Yuck," I said.

"Give it a try. I'll bet it's fun," said my Mom.

"It'll be good for you," said my Dad.

"Awwwwww," I said.

"Eat your glop, dear," they said. I did, but it didn't taste as good anymore.

I was grumpy the next morning. When Maggie came out for school, she was even grumpier.

"Cyril," she said, "The most terrible thing that ever happened to me has happened. I have to take piano lessons." She booted a stone down the street.

"You think that's bad?" I said. "I have to take floor hockey."

"Ever lucky!" said Maggie. "That's what I wanted."

"Am not," I said. "I wanted piano."

We walked a little further and Maggie said, "Why don't we trade? You take piano for me, and I'll play floor hockey for you."

"How can we do that?" I asked.

"Easy. We'll just switch places. Nobody will know. You can sneak over and use the piano in our basement, and I can play all the hockey I want." Maggie got all excited making plans as we walked down Greenapple Street.

"We'll get in trouble," I said.

"Come on, Cyril," Maggie said. "Partners help each other, right? And we're partners."

"Yes, but..." I began.

"I bet Ugly Augie Crumley signs up for floor hockey."

"Okay, let's trade," I said.

And that's what we did. The first Saturday morning, I told the piano teacher that "Maggie" was supposed to be "Maxie." Maggie told the floor hockey instructor that "Cyril" was supposed to be "Cheryl." Nobody told on me because none of my friends took piano. Nobody told on Maggie because all the kids wanted her on their team.

When it was time to go home, I gave Maggie her piano book. She gave me my running shoes.

"Thanks to me," she said, "you got four goals and three assists. What a star! Your parents won't believe it. What did I learn?"

"Where to find middle C, how to hold your fingers, and a song called "Up and Down." It has three notes and I—I mean you—can almost play it already."

I was so proud of myself that I wanted to start playing Maggie's piano right away. After lunch, I snuck over to Maggie's. She let me in the side door and we slipped down into the basement.

"I'm practising now, so start timing," she yelled upstairs. Then she closed the door.

"Play loud," said Maggie. "I said I was nervous so my parents promised not to look, but they'll be listening for sure. And make it good. It's supposed to be a genius playing the piano, remember?" She flopped on the sofa and opened a book.

I sat down at the piano. It was a lot nicer and newer than the one at school. The wood smelled fresh and a little mysterious—like a treasure chest would smell. The keys gleamed black and white. They were so clean that I didn't want to touch them at first.

Softly I pressed a key. It sank under my finger, and a note boomed out loud enough to blow the house down. Nobody seemed to notice. I put my fingers in the right place and tried again. This time it didn't sound so loud. It sounded good. Soon I forgot all about where I was and just kept playing "Up and Down" until I had it perfect.

There were thumping noises.

"Time's up!" called a voice, and I was bumped off the piano bench.

"Hide!" Maggie hissed. "It's my Dad." I dove behind the couch.

The door opened. "Sounded great," said Maggie's Dad. "Didn't I say you'd like it?"

"Yes, Dad," Maggie said.

He went off whistling "Up and Down." I crawled out from behind the couch.

"It worked," said Maggie. "Alright, what a plan!" We traded high fives, then we snuck outside and spent the afternoon playing hockey in the driveway.

At dinner that night, I pretended I got Maggie's goals and assists at floor hockey. My parents thought I was going to be a superstar. We had chocolate glop for dessert.

In just three weeks, Maggie got seventeen goals and nineteen assists. She started to say floor hockey was too easy, and maybe real hockey would be better. I learned five new songs and began playing the piano with both hands. My teacher said I had the makings of a real musician.

Our parents thought it was the other way around, and everybody was happy. I was always getting chocolate glop.

Then the problem began. Now that Maggie was supposed to be so good at piano, she started to bug me when I was practising. She began standing beside me and fussing every time I made a mistake.

The worst thing was that nobody would ever know I was the one at the piano no matter how well I played. It was no fun at all.

Nothing was fun anymore. Practising the piano wasn't fun. Playing hockey in the driveway wasn't fun because I always lost. Thinking about winter wasn't fun. After a while, even chocolate glop wasn't fun anymore.

Finally, one Monday right in the middle of practising I said, "I quit. I don't want to do this anymore."

"You can't quit," said Maggie. "I made a plan. We made a deal."

"I don't care," I said. "I quit."

"Okay, smarty," said Maggie. "See if I help you anymore. Go play hockey yourself."

"See if I care," I said. "Play your own piano," and I went home.

For the next two days, I was so mad at Maggie I forgot to think about floor hockey. Saturday seemed a long way away. Besides, it felt good not being bossed and not sneaking around. Sneaking really tired me out after a while.

Then, at dinner on Wednesday, my mother said, "We're invited to a block party at Maggie's on Friday night, Cyril. Won't that be nice? Maggie's mother tells me that Maggie is going to give a little concert on the piano. I hear she's doing very well at her lessons."

I nearly choked on my mashed potatoes.

"Are you all right?" asked my Dad.

41

"Uh-huh," I said. I put my napkin up to my face to hide a big grin. There was no way she could get out of this one. Maggie was sunk.

Or was she? She was pretty smart. What if she did get out of it? Then I thought about how much I missed the piano. I should be the one playing on Friday night. Now I might never have a chance to play again.

The telephone rang as I was helping with the dishes. It was Maggie. She tried to sound tough, but I could tell she was scared.

"I wouldn't call you usually, Cyril, since you're a deal-wrecker. But I've decided to give you another chance," she snapped.

"Forget it," I said. "I don't need another chance. You do. I've already heard about Friday."

"Aren't we still partners?" asked Maggie. She didn't sound as mean now.

"Maybe," I said.

"Come on, Cyril, we're best friends." Now Maggie was talking like I was the nicest person in the world.

"It depends," I said. "You'll have to do everything I say."

"What?" she screeched. "No way! You little..."

"Okay, 'bye," I said. "See you Friday."

"Wait a sec," Maggie said, very fast. "We can

make a deal. If you teach me piano, I'll teach you hockey."

My mom came into the room.

"No," I whispered. "I'll teach you piano, but I get to do my practising, and you have to keep on playing hockey for me."

She was stuck and she knew it. "Okay," she grumbled.

"Good," I said, "We start tomorrow after school." I hung up the phone feeling terrific. The whole thing had been easy.

Things got harder, fast. When I tried to teach her, Maggie complained that piano was boring. She didn't listen at all.

"I don't have to start at the beginning," she said. "Just show me one song for Friday." Then she picked "Mysterious Melody," the hardest one. It sounded like she was hitting the keys with her feet when she tried it.

"That's enough," I said. "You just can't play the piano."

"Then what am I going to do?" Maggie asked.

"How about putting on a record and pretending to play?" I suggested.

Maggie thought. "I don't think that will work," she said. Then a gleam came into her eyes. "But if we were real partners again, you could play the piano for me."

"Huh?"

"You could wear a disguise," said Maggie. "As long as they can't tell who's playing, they'll think I am." She paused. "And if you do this for me, I'll fix it so you won't have to worry about floor hockey anymore."

"What will you do?" I asked.

"Just trust me," Maggie said. "It'll work."

That sounded pretty good. I did want to play the piano for a bunch of people, and Maggie was going to do something for me.

"Okay," I said. "We're partners, as long as I can help with the disguise."

"Sure," said Maggie. "We'll start as soon as you finish practising, partner."

On Friday night everyone on Greenapple Street came to Maggie's with barbecues and stuff to eat. We brought hamburgers and chocolate glop. I was so excited I only had one hamburger and saved my glop.

While I was eating, I saw Maggie talking to Mr. Birney, the man who runs Half-Pint Hockey. I hope she knows what she's doing, I thought. I sure don't want to play real hockey. When they stopped talking, Maggie came over to me.

"Disguise time," she said. We went to the basement to get started.

First, Maggie taped two hockey pucks to the

bottom of my shoes to make me taller. Then we cut two eye holes in an old bed sheet and put it over my head. On top of that, I put on some glasses with a big nose and a moustache attached to them. Then Maggie got a baseball cap and pulled it down on my head to keep the sheet from moving around.

As we worked, Maggie said, "I told my Mom I was going to wear a costume to go with the song. She thinks I'm dressing up, not disguising. Now, stick out your arms."

I couldn't see very well with all the stuff on my head, so at first I didn't know what she was doing. Then I felt her loading my arms with junky old bracelets.

"Hey! I didn't pick that stuff!" I said.

"Hold still," said Maggie. "We forgot. Disguising your arms and hands is the most important part." Then she put nail polish on me.

"Eeeewwwww, yuck," I said.

"Ssshhh," she said, "Shake them dry."

I shook. The bracelets clanked and jangled. I felt stupid. Right then I was glad there was a sheet over my head.

Maggie steered me to the laundry room door.

"Now, when everybody goes into the recreation room, you walk in, go to the piano, and play the song. Don't say a word. Then come back to the door, turn around, and take a big bow. Then I'll get you out of hockey and me out of piano.

"Oh, and if I'm not around later, I'll be out in the driveway."

In the next room, we could hear everybody coming in.

Maggie's Mom said, "It's time for me to introduce a mysterious piano player who's going to play a 'Mysterious Melody'."

Maggie gave me a shove, and I clomped into the room. There was laughing and clapping as I went to the piano. The hockey pucks were really hard to walk on. I had to hold the sheet up, and it twisted around and made it hard to see.

I bumped into a chair and said, "Ow." A hand steadied me. It was my Dad's!

"Ow," I said again, trying to sound like Maggie.

My Dad stared at me hard, and I clomped away fast.

I got to the piano bench, tugged my sheet up, and climbed on. It took a second to find middle C. I put my fingers on the keys. All the bracelets rattled down my arms and piled up at my wrists. I shook them back. For the first time, I saw that Maggie had painted my fingernails purple.

It got very quiet, and suddenly I got very scared. My hands felt all wet. I wanted to wipe them on the sheet, but I couldn't move. The keys on the piano didn't make any sense at all. I knew

I was going to make a mistake. What song was I supposed to play? I couldn't remember anything.

Then a chair creaked right behind me, and I jumped. My fingers hit the keys. I began playing "Mysterious Melody" faster than I'd ever played it before, bracelets jingling and purple fingers flashing. I played it twice before I remembered it was supposed to end. The next time through I stopped.

Everybody clapped. Someone yelled "Bravo" and whistled.

I slid off the bench while everybody was still clapping and shuffled to the door. My hockey pucks were clomping. My sheet was flapping. My glasses were bouncing, and all those clunky bracelets were jangling. I was just glad it was over.

By the wall, my Mom and Dad were whispering to each other and looking at me. I got a little nervous.

But everybody kept on clapping, so I slowed down and waved, just like they do on TV. By the time I got to the door, I was so proud I was wishing they could all see who it really was, even if I did look funny.

"Take a bow! Take off the hat, and take a bow!" Maggie whispered from outside the door. I deserved it. I twisted around to face everyone, swept off the baseball cap, and bowed low to the ground.

I felt a tug from behind. The glasses with the nose and moustache tumbled off. The sheet disappeared between my feet. All that was left was me, with bracelets and purple fingernails, wobbling around on two hockey pucks.

"Cyril!" gasped Maggie's parents.

"Cyril!" said the neighbours.

"I thought so!" said my Dad.

I whirled around. Maggie and the sheet were gone. I had been tricked, and now I was trapped. I felt my face get very red and bowed to hide it. People laughed and clapped all over again.

"Great playing, Cyril," they said.

"What a cute trick."

"A born performer."

"I bet you're proud of him!"

My parents said they were. I wasn't so sure. My parents and Maggie's acted like they knew what was going on all the time, until everybody had gone upstairs.

"Cyril, wherever did you learn to play the piano?" asked my Mom.

"I don't know." I squirmed.

"You don't know?" said my Dad. I could tell from his voice he didn't believe me. Neither did anyone else. There was no reason to pretend any longer, so I told them.

"On Saturdays. At community school," I said. "I practised over here."

"You mean that was you playing every day?" asked Maggie's Dad. "Then what was Maggie doing all this time?"

"Playing floor hockey," I said. "She has fifty-seven goals and forty-six assists."

Then I told them all about how we had traded. At first they didn't believe me. Then they looked pretty angry. Then they looked like they couldn't choose between laughing and getting mad.

"Where's Maggie now?" asked her Mom.

"She told me she'd be in the driveway," I said.

"We're going to talk more about this later, Cyril," said my Dad.

We went upstairs. Maggie and Mr. Birney were in the driveway playing hockey. Maggie was wearing a hockey sweater and taking shots on Mr. Birney in goal. A bunch of people were watching them. Maggie took a slapshot and scored. Mr. Birney looked a little red in the face.

"Sign her up," someone said. "First girl in the league."

"I'm going to be," said Maggie, "if my parents let me."

"If she skates as well as she shoots, she'll be fine," said Mr. Birney.

Maggie's Mom and Dad looked at each other.

"Why don't we all talk it over?" her Mom said.

Maggie started taking shots again. My parents whispered behind me. Then my Dad leaned over.

"You really want to take piano, do you, Cyril?" he asked.

"Yes, Dad," I said.

"Then your mother and I think that's what you'd better take. Maggie's parents will let you practise here for a while longer. You should be all rested up for your practising too, because you're going to be skipping TV and going to bed early to make up for some tall tales you've been telling about hockey."

"Yes, Dad. Thanks, Dad." I felt better all of a sudden.

My Dad still seemed disappointed, so I said, "At least you won't have to take me to practise at five o'clock in the morning."

"That's true," he said.

Mr. Birney made a big save with his glove. We both clapped.

"Don't you like hockey, Cyril?" my Dad asked.

"Sure," I said. "I like to watch it lots. I like to play it sometimes. I just play piano better."

"Maybe you do at that," said my Dad.

Maggie looked over. I smiled and nodded. She winked and stickhandled in on Mr. Birney. Maggie's pretty smart, I thought. I just hope she likes getting up at five o'clock in the morning.

Then I went to get my chocolate glop. I felt like I'd earned it.

50

Crime Wave in Room 7

It was the worst kind of day. The sun was shining, we had the afternoon off school, and still nothing was right. My best tennis ball was missing.

It was the best tennis ball in the whole world. All the fuzz had come off a long time ago. Now it was grey with black stripes where I had marked it with a felt pen. It was smooth and so soft you could squeeze it in your fingers—just right for throwing and catching. Something mysterious rattled inside when you shook it. It was the perfect ball, and it was gone.

I looked all over the house and the yard, but there was no tennis ball. The only place left to look was the school yard. I didn't think it was there, but it felt better to keep looking than to give up.

There was no tennis ball in the school yard, but I did find a blue mini-football. I kept it and went over to look in the playground.

Monica was sitting on the jungle gym watching Bobby Devlin show off on the swings. Bobby was blowing a huge bubble with grape bubble gum as he swung. You could smell it a mile away.

"Hi, Cyril," said Monica.

"Hi," I said. I started looking in the sandbox.

"What are you doing?" Monica asked.

"Looking for my tennis ball," I said. "I can't find it anywhere."

"I can't find my jumpsies rope either," Monica said. "It's gone, and it was 83 elastics long. Have you seen it?"

"No," I said. "Have you seen my tennis ball?"

Monica shook her head.

"Hey, Bobby," I called, "have you seen my tennis ball?"

Bobby didn't answer. He was blowing a big bubble and couldn't talk.

"Or a jumpsies rope?" asked Monica.

Bobby sucked his bubble in and slowed down his swing.

When he stopped, he said, "No, but I lost a black pen with an airplane that flies up and down when you tip it. Have you seen that?"

"No," we said.

"I had it at school yesterday, and now it's gone."

We all thought about what we had lost.

Monica said, "It's pretty strange, all that stuff disappearing."

Bobby nodded. "It's pretty suspicious—just like it was stolen."

"Stolen! Do you think so?" I had never thought of that.

"Yup," said Bobby as he cracked another bubble.

"What'll we do?" asked Monica.

Bobby started to huff and puff, but before he said anything, I said, "We should tell Maggie. She'll think of something."

"Maggie!" Bobby snorted. He didn't like Maggie because she could beat him at floor hockey.

"Yeah, Maggie. She's a genius. She can solve this." Besides, Maggie and I were partners.

"Come on, Bobby," Monica said.

"Okay," he grumbled.

Maggie was in her tree house when we arrived. She came down, and I told her that we had been robbed.

"Can you find who did it?" Monica asked.

"Of course I can," said Maggie.

"Sure," said Bobby.

"If you do everything I say," Maggie said.

"Okay," said Monica right away. She didn't know what that could mean.

I said, "I don't have to. We're partners."

Maggie shook her head. "Not this time, Cyril. You asked for help."

"Aw," I said, "...okay." I really wanted my tennis ball.

Then we looked at Bobby. He pretended to bow.

"Yes, master. This I've got to see," he snickered.

Maggie ignored him. "Now," she said, "you have to ask all the other kids if they're missing anything. If they are, tell them to come here tomorrow after school."

Maggie was getting excited. "This might be a crime wave. Wouldn't that be fantastic?" she said.

The next day, there was a line-up at Maggie's tree. Nearly everybody from Mr. Flynn's class was there. Some kids from Ms. Elrod's class came too. George was there, and so were Lester, Karina, Bobby, and Monica. Maggie and I sat up in the tree house, and Maggie called them up one at a time. She asked the questions, and I had to write down the answers.

The first one up was Lester. His pencil case was gone. I wrote down what it looked like and when it disappeared and where.

"If everybody's being robbed," Lester said, "I bet it's cat burglars, maybe a whole gang."

"Maybe," said Maggie. "That's all for now."

"That's it?" said Lester, "Aren't we going to chase them or anything?"

"Not right now," said Maggie. "But Cyril will call you when we do. Send up the next person when you get down."

Lester looked pretty disappointed, but he climbed down.

Soon I had a huge list of missing things. There were balls and pens, fold-up erasers, key chains and pencil cases, charm chains, skipping ropes, robots, sticker books, toy cars. People suspected best friends, brothers and sisters, aliens, crooks, and Ugly Augie Crumley.

Just then, Ugly Augie climbed into the tree house.

"Ah ha!" I said. "Here to confess?" I felt pretty brave now that Maggie and I were partners most of the time.

"None of your beeswax," said Crumley. "I want to talk to her."

"It's okay, Crumley," Maggie said. "Cyril's helping."

Ugly Augie said, "Somebody stole something from me."

Who cares, I thought, but Maggie said, "Uh-huh."

"Think you can find it?" asked Ugly Augie.

"With my eyes closed," said Maggie. "What's missing?"

For a minute, Ugly Augie didn't say anything.

He just stared at the floor. Then his face turned very red and his voice got very quiet.

"A teddy bear," he said. "But it wasn't mine. It's my little sister's. Sometimes I carry it for her."

I could hardly write, I was giggling so hard, but Maggie didn't say a word.

As Crumley was leaving, I said, "Hey Crumley, I should have put poison ivy on your teddy bear."

For a second, I thought he was going to slug me. Then Maggie said, "Cut it out, Cyril. You don't talk like that to clients."

"Lucky for you," Crumley growled, and he climbed down.

"How many are left to see?" asked Maggie.

I looked.

"Four," I said.

"Okay," she said. "I'll finish here. You go down and get the ball of string and the bag of tin cans from my garage."

So I climbed down as George climbed up. And that's why everything turned out the way it did later on.

The next morning, when I called for Maggie, her mother told me she'd already left. I raced down Greenapple Street to look for her in the school yard. But she wasn't there either.

I went inside and down the long, empty hall to Room 7. It was so early that no one was supposed to be there. When I got to Room 7, there was Maggie. She was standing with her back to the door looking at something on Monica's desk. In her hand, was the list of things that had been stolen.

"Hey," I said.

"Get lost, Cyril," she hissed. "I'm busy."

"Why? What are you doing? Are you solving the case?"

"Maybe," she said. "Now go away."

I tried to see what she had on the desk.

"I thought we were partners," I said.

She said, "Not this time, remember? But if you really want to help, stand guard at the door and warn me if anyone comes."

It was better than doing nothing. I went to the door and looked out. Nobody was around. Behind me chairs scraped, papers rustled, pencils clattered. It sounded like Maggie was searching all the desks. Once or twice she giggled and said, "Wow."

What was she doing? I turned around to peek. Maggie was stuffing something into a paper bag.

"You two are here bright and early this morning," said Mr. Flynn, right behind me. I jumped.

"Yes, sir," said Maggie. "I just wanted to put my bag in my desk."

"Okay, then it's outside until the bell." Mr. Flynn went to his own desk, and we went outside.

"Some lookout you were," Maggie said.

"Sorry," I said. "But what were you doing anyway?"

Maggie smiled as if she knew a fantastic secret and walked away. I gritted my teeth. I hated to be left out, and Maggie knew it.

At lunch time, Maggie took the bag home. I watched her house, and after lunch I followed her back to school early. If Maggie wasn't going to tell me what she was doing, I'd find out for myself.

I hurried to the windows. Maggie was in Room 7, poking at the shelves over the coat hooks. She took a paper bag out of her pocket and put something in it. Then she came toward the window. I ducked. After a while, she went to Ms. Elrod's class and did the same thing.

She's investigating, I told myself. But what? The scene of the crimes, I thought. After all, nearly everyone's stuff vanished at school. Then what was she putting in the bag? Evidence, I told myself. But what kind? My stomach started to feel uneasy.

The door by the kindergarten opened, and Maggie came out. She stopped when she saw me.

"Hi, Cyril," she said. "I forgot to take my bag home at lunch, so I'm taking it now."

Maggie ran off.

The uneasy feeling got worse. Something was very wrong, and I had to know what it was. I had to look in the school myself.

There was no one around as I opened the door and slipped inside. I waited. Nothing happened, so I took a deep breath and shot down the hall.

Room 7 was cool and dim with the lights off. You could hear kids yelling in the playground outside.

I went to my desk. It looked the same to me. Except... I looked again. Sure enough, my mini-football was gone. Before I could stop it, a terrible thought leaped into my mind. Had Maggie stolen my football? Was she taking things from people's desks? Was Maggie a thief? *The* thief? The best-friend part of me said "no," but my brain said "yes."

Then the bell clanged like a burglar alarm. I shrieked. Down the hall came the sound of voices and hurrying feet. Unless I moved fast, I was going to get caught all alone in a classroom where I wasn't supposed to be—a classroom where stuff was getting stolen.

I looked around frantically. Then I leaped behind the door and held my breath as everybody burst into the classroom. Just as I got ready to slip out, the door swung away from me.

"Going to join us, Cyril?" Mr. Flynn glanced at me as he closed the door.

The more I thought about it, the worse everything seemed. I was even the dummy who told everybody Maggie could help! I didn't know what to do. All afternoon, Maggie acted as if nothing was wrong. She even got perfect in spelling. I was so worried I almost failed.

After school, we all went back to the tree house. Everyone had been robbed again. Maggie came into the yard smiling her secret smile and carrying another brown bag. Everybody started talking at once.

"I thought you were solving this," screeched Bobby Devlin.

Crumley just growled.

"Hold it," Maggie said. "Come up one at a time and tell me."

I went first. I climbed up not knowing what to say. How do you tell your best friend that you think she's a thief?

I decided just to hint. I looked Maggie right in the eye and said, "Somebody stole my mini-football today." She looked as if she was going to laugh.

"What's so funny?" I asked.

"Nothing," she said.

Slowly I told her about the football in my desk. She pretended to cough to keep from laughing, then wrote it all down.

I looked around. In the top corner of the tree house, a bulging shopping bag hung from a nail. Maggie smiled.

I started to get mad. She wasn't sorry at all, and

she was laughing at me because she thought I was dumb.

"I want you to do something for me," she said.

That did it. I didn't want to help anybody steal anything.

I said, "Sorry, I'm going to have dinner early tonight." Some friend you are, I thought.

I went home feeling madder and madder. I had done everything but tell Maggie I knew she was stealing. All she did was laugh. If that was how she was going to be, I'd get some proof and tell everybody. Then we'd see who the dummy was. By the time I got home, I had a plan.

I waited until Maggie went in for supper, then I headed for the tree in her backyard. I knew that nobody could see me from Maggie's kitchen. I had to get a look in that bag.

It was scary sneaking around there. I had a feeling that Maggie might get me somehow. I climbed over the thread that Maggie always stretched across the doorway when she left. If it was broken, she knew someone had been there.

Then I tried to pull the shopping bag down, but it was caught on a piece of string. Suddenly, from a way off, I heard the noise of tin cans clanking together. I looked at the string and tugged again. More clanking—it was an alarm.

There was no time to lose. I pulled the bag down and looked inside. It was a treasure chest.

Nearly everything that had been stolen was there.

A door slammed below, and footsteps thudded across the yard.

"Who's there?" Maggie called. "You'd better come down. That tree is booby-trapped!"

I began to rub the top of my head and moan. I looked out the door.

"Cyril!" said Maggie. "What are you doing up there?"

"Looking...owwww...for my homework. I thought I left it up here, and I hit my head on some stupid bag."

"Oh," said Maggie. "Well, it's not here."

I climbed down to the ground.

"Let me see your head," said Maggie. She started to push my hair around.

"You're not getting a bump or anything," she said suspiciously.

"It sure feels like I am," I lied.

Maggie didn't say anything.

"Well," I said, "see you tomorrow."

"See you," said Maggie.

I knew she was watching me as I walked away. It was hard to keep from running. When I got to my house, I turned around. Maggie was climbing into the tree house. She suspected something for sure.

Now I had to act fast—before Maggie got away and before anyone else figured things out. No one would believe I wasn't helping Maggie and I'd be in trouble too. I shuddered all over. Two close calls in one day, and I still had a lot to do. Maybe detective work wasn't for me.

I watched the tree house until bedtime. Maggie didn't bring the bag with her when she came down. The next morning, I made sure she didn't take it with her to school.

Then I started passing the message, "Maggie says not to say anything to anyone, even her, but the case is solved. Come to her place after school."

At lunch time, I watched the tree house. Nothing changed. My plan was going to work.

After school, I led a crowd to the tree house. We all waited for Maggie. After a while, she came into the yard carrying another paper bag. She didn't seem surprised at all.

"Just the people I wanted to see," she cried. "The case is solved."

"We know," Lester said. "Cyril already told us."

"He did?" said Maggie. "Did he tell you all about it?"

"He was waiting for you," said Monica.

"Well, now I'm here," said Maggie. "You tell, Cyril. I want to put my bag in the tree house."

I gave her a last chance. "Are you sure you want me to?" I asked.

"Yup," said Maggie. She began to climb. Everybody moved in close.

I took a deep breath and asked, "What would you do if I said that yesterday before school I saw somebody looking in people's desks?"

"Pound 'em," said Ugly Augie.

"And what if I told you I saw the same person in Mr. Flynn's class and Ms. Elrod's putting stuff in a paper bag?"

"I'd double pound 'em," yelled Ugly Augie.

"Yeah," echoed Bobby.

The crowd moved closer.

"And what if this person saw me and lied to me about what *she* was doing?" I said that part really loud.

"Triple pound 'em," shouted Ugly Augie and a few others.

"And what if I saw this same person take this paper bag up Greenapple Street? And what if I said that all the stolen stuff is hidden very close to here? And that I know because I saw it? And what if I said that the person who stole it is very, very smart? And what if I said that the thief is..."

"Maggie!" Crumley screamed. "I knew it! Get her!"

The crowd rushed to the tree, Crumley in the lead. Suddenly there was a squishing noise, and Ugly Augie was drenched with water. A broken water balloon lay at his feet. Monica screamed. The crowd looked up and froze.

"Everybody stay right where you are," said

64

Maggie. She was standing in the doorway of the tree house. A huge red water balloon wobbled in her hands.

"The first balloon had water," she said. "This one is filled with paint. And there's lots more where this came from. First one to touch the tree gets it."

The crowd took a step back.

"I'm only going to say this once," said Maggie, "so pay attention. Cyril doesn't know the whole story. I did sneak into school and take things, and I did lie to Cyril. Sorry, Cyril."

"That's okay," I said, without thinking.

"Robber!" yelled Bobby Devlin.

"Watch it, motormouth," said Maggie. She lifted the balloon.

"Cyril did find the stuff," Maggie continued. "I know because he set off an alarm. He almost fooled me. The bag was hanging too high for you to bump your head, Cyril. Nice try though."

"Thanks," I said. When Maggie said something was good, you knew it was good, even if she was a criminal.

"What's with you?" roared Bobby. "Are you in on it too?"

Maggie said, "Sure he is."

"No I'm not," I said very fast.

"Yes he is," said Maggie. "So is Monica, and Lester, and George, and Karina, and...everybody. Even you, Bobby Devlin."

Everybody started yelling at once.

65

Maggie roared, "Somebody's going to get it!"
Everybody stopped.

"I'll prove it," said Maggie. Gently she lowered the balloon. She lifted the shopping bag and pulled something out.

"Who does this belong to?" she asked.

It was my mini-football.

Before I could say anything, George yelled, "That's mine!"

Maggie said, "But Cyril says it's his."

"What a thief! It is not," said George. "Somebody stole it four days ago. I told you."

Suddenly I remembered George climbing up to the tree house as I climbed down. I got very scared.

"But Cyril found it in the school yard," Maggie said. "That means you lost it and Cyril found it without knowing it was yours."

"Yes," I said.

"Here." Maggie threw the ball to George. "Let's try another one."

She lifted a black pen with an airplane that moved back and forth in one end.

"Whose?" she asked.

"Mine," yelled Bobby and Lester and Karina all at once.

"Bobby says it was stolen three days ago. Lester told me it was stolen yesterday. What makes you think it's yours, Lester?" asked Maggie.

"I found it fair and square at the drinking fountain," Lester said. "I didn't know it was his."

"Then give it here," said Bobby.

"But," said Maggie, "Karina lost it four days ago, and you said it was brand new, Bobby. Where did you get it?"

"Well, it was...like...just on a chair in the class," stammered Bobby. I didn't know it belonged...like...to anybody."

"Now you do," said Maggie. The pen went back to Karina. Maggie reached for something else.

Just about everybody got back what had been lost. Most of the stuff had been picked up by kids who found it lying around. Maggie said it belonged to whoever lost it first.

Finally, people began to go home until just Maggie, Ugly Augie, and I were left.

"Crumley," said Maggie. "I almost forgot."

She handed him something in a paper bag. He looked inside and started to grin. Then he stopped. His face got very red, and he closed the bag.

"Well, uh...thanks," he said. "See you."

As he walked past me, he said, "Thought you were pretty smart, didn't you?" He laughed once and went away.

I was feeling a lot of things at once. I was glad Maggie was my friend again and not a criminal. I felt a little dumb and mad about being tricked.

But mainly I was happy it was all over.

"Did you see my great shot with that water balloon?" Maggie asked me.

"Was there really paint inside some of them?" I asked.

"No," said Maggie, "but with coloured balloons, who can tell?"

"Sorry about saying you stole everything," I said.

"I did, sort of," said Maggie. "I was going to tell you yesterday, but you said you had an early dinner. Before that, I wasn't sure."

Maybe, I thought, and maybe you just wanted to be a big hero and surprise everybody.

"How did you figure it out?" I asked.

"Easy," she said. "I knew as soon as Monica said she lost her jumpsies rope because I found that a week ago. I was going to tell her right away, but then I thought the same thing might have happened to all the stuff. If I found it, what a great surprise that would make. So I kept quiet."

"You sure did," I said. "You didn't even tell Monica today that you were the one who took her rope."

"Well, you can't tell everything, Cyril," said Maggie.

"What did you give Crumley?" I asked.

"His teddy bear," said Maggie. "Crumley's little sister had it hidden in the kindergarten. That was the only real theft in the whole bunch."

"But why didn't you tell everybody?" I asked. "You could really have got Crumley."

"Like I said, Cyril, you don't tell everything. Besides, this way he owes me a favour." Maggie smiled.

"There's just one other thing," I said. "What about my tennis ball? I never got it back."

Maggie shook her head. "I don't know Cyril. That's one thing I never found. It's still a mystery, I guess."

So I went home with no tennis ball and no football either. I was fed up with mysteries and crimes. I was the only person who'd lost out.

When I walked into my room, I couldn't believe my eyes. There was my tennis ball lying right on my bed. I raced downstairs to the front door.

"You're awfully happy all of a sudden," my Mom called.

"Look. I found my tennis ball," I said. "I've been searching all over for it, and now I just found it on my bed. Weird, huh?"

"Have you been looking for that, dear?" asked my mother. "I'm sorry. I borrowed it a day or two ago to put it in the clothes dryer. I washed your down jacket and the ball bounces around and helps it dry faster." She smiled. "I was going to tell you, but I guess I forgot."

"Really," I said.

"I hope you weren't too worried," said my mother.

I almost told her, but then I squeezed my tennis ball, I could already feel myself bouncing it off the garage door.

"It's okay," I said—and it was.

The Best Tree
You Can Be

Christmas was coming, but you couldn't tell. All it ever did was rain, and rain didn't make me feel like Christmas. It just made me feel soggy.

As I trudged down Greenapple Street on my way to school, I felt as cold and grey as the sky. The street lights were still glowing, but nothing looked any brighter. Everything looked dull. It was the kind of time that made you really wish for something special to happen.

When I got to school, everybody seemed to have something special about them except me. Monica Goodman had new red boots. Ugly Augie Crumley didn't have to wear boots. Bobby Devlin had a neat ski jacket. Lester and George were staying for lunch. Some kids were going swimming. Others were telling secrets or winning games. Some even had ear muffs and snowmobile gloves.

I had a plain old jacket and plain old boots and a plain old hat with a dumb red pom-pom that

71

everybody laughed at. I still had mittens on a string. I wasn't going anywhere or doing anything. I was just plain old Cyril.

Over by the doors, Maggie was telling a riddle.

"What do you call a lion that walks across the desert?" she asked

Nobody could guess.

"Sandy Claws," she said. Everybody groaned as the bell rang. I plodded down the hall to Room 7. I didn't know any riddles either.

It wasn't until that afternoon that I found out how I could be special too. Instead of doing spelling, our teacher, Mr. Flynn, sat down at the front of his desk. He brushed up his moustache until the ends nearly poked into his eyes. That meant he had an announcement.

When everybody was quiet, he said, "Room 7 has been asked to put on the Christmas assembly. We are going to perform a play."

Everybody started talking at once, and right then I knew the way I wanted to be special. I wanted to be the star of the Christmas assembly.

"We have four weeks to get ready," said Mr. Flynn, "and there's a lot to do. Some people will make scenery and help backstage, some will sing in the choir, and some will be actors. You'll all have a chance to choose what you want to do."

Mr. Flynn drew a red circle around December 17 on the calendar. That was the night we were going to put on our play for all the students and their families. Then he called out our names, one at a time, and asked what we wanted to do.

"Actor," I said.

"Backstage helper," said Maggie. "I want to run the lights," she whispered to me.

When he was finished, Mr. Flynn said, "There'll be try-outs for all the acting parts tomorrow."

Try-outs? I never thought of that. I just thought I was going to be a star.

"How do we try out?" I asked.

"You have to act a little bit of the part for us," said Mr. Flynn.

"Will everybody be watching?" I asked. I hadn't thought of that either.

"That's what acting is all about," Mr. Flynn said. "Don't worry. There'll be a part for everyone."

But I wanted more than any old part, and trying out sounded scary. I asked Maggie to help me.

"It'll be easy as pie," she said. "I'll make you a star. But, you'll..."

"Have to do everything I say," I finished for her.

"Yup," said Maggie, "and do my Christmas shopping for me."

It was worth it to be a star. We made a deal.

Maggie said the first thing to do was to make me look like a star.

"That way," she said, "it doesn't matter if you

can act or not. If you look cool, everyone will think you're great.''

We cut a big label off her Mom's jeans and glued it onto mine. I got my Dad's special black shirt with the red and purple flowers all over it, and Maggie pinned it so it fit me. Then we got gold chains for around my neck and slicked back my hair with gooey stuff. Maggie found a pair of big black sunglasses, and I tried them on. That night, I practised looking cool.

The next morning, I was special as soon as I took my plain old coat off. Everybody stared. I pretended I was too cool to notice. I put on my sunglasses, tilted my head back, opened my mouth, and put my hands in my pockets. It was hard to sit at my desk that way.

Mr. Flynn came in.

''We have a busy day today, so let's get started...Uh, Cyril, do you have a sore neck?''

''No, sir,'' I said.

''Are your eyes bothering you?''

''No, sir.''

''Would you sit up then please, and take your sunglasses off in class?''

''Yes sir.'' It was harder to look cool this way. A couple of kids giggled.

Try-out time arrived. All the actors went to the gym to use the stage.

''Think Hollywood,'' Maggie whispered. I put my sunglasses back on.

We tried out for Santa Claus first. Each actor had to walk out and look at the clock, say "It's Christmas Eve and I'm late HoHoHo," pretend to pick up a big bag of toys, and walk off.

George went first. He was too fast. Lester forgot what to say. Monica giggled when she tried. Bobby Devlin did okay.

Then I tried. It was hard being a cool Santa Claus.

"I said, "Hey, it's Christmas Eve and I'm late, HoHo..." and bent down to pick up the bag of toys. One of the pins in my shirt pricked me from behind.

"Hooooooo." I jumped and everybody laughed.

"Thank you, Cyril," said Mr. Flynn.

Bobby Devlin got to be Santa Claus.

Lester got to be the snowman. He melted really well. While I was melting, the label started falling off my jeans. I had to keep slapping it back on my rear end.

"Thank you, Cyril," said Mr. Flynn.

George got to be the narrator. Just before my turn, I tried to take my chains off, and they stuck around my head. It was hard to speak clearly with chains wrapped around my nose.

"Thank you, Cyril," said Mr. Flynn.

I didn't get to be the snow fairy either. Monica got that. With my sunglasses on, I couldn't see that my shoelace was untied, and I tripped when

I was supposed to tiptoe behind the snowman. Instead of breaking the magic spell, I knocked him over.

"Thank you, Cyril," said Mr. Flynn.

I tried out for everything. I didn't get to be one of the children, or one of the elves, or one of the mice, or one of the reindeer. I got to be a tree—a tree in the middle of the forest. I had to stand there holding my arms out like branches and watch everybody else be special.

After all the parts were handed out, I sat down by myself in a corner of the gym.

"Stupid play," I said to myself. "Who cares? It'll stink anyway." For some reason, I felt like I was going to cry.

"You had some trouble this afternoon, eh Cyril?" Mr. Flynn sat down beside me.

"Yes, sir," I sniffled and looked away. Nobody was going to see me crying.

"Even though you didn't get a big part, you can still have fun," said Mr. Flynn.

I said, "Yes, sir." But I didn't see how.

"People can be the biggest stars in the world," said Mr. Flynn, "but they won't look very good unless all the actors in all the parts do their best. If you'll be the best tree you can be, Cyril, good things will happen to you and this play. Will you do that for me and everybody else?"

"Yes, sir," I said.

"Good," he said. "See you at practice tomorrow."

But Maggie had promised to make me a star.

"It didn't work at all," I told her. "I'm just a dumb old tree."

"Don't worry," said Maggie. "I promised to make you a star, and I'll make you one."

"How?" I asked.

"Never mind for now," she whispered. "I can't tell you my new incredible idea yet."

"Because you don't have one," I said.

"I'll have one," she said. "You wait and see. Just be the best tree you can be for now, and make sure to keep some time for my Christmas shopping."

I set out to be the best tree I could be. I practised standing still. I practised holding my arms out like branches. I practised looking enchanted. Nobody noticed, but I knew I was going to be a star somehow.

At the right time in the play, all the trees had to sneak onstage while the curtains were closed and make the enchanted forest. Then the lights went out. As the curtains opened, we made whooshing noises to sound like the wind howling. When the lights came on, we waved our branches back and forth.

Then Ms. Elrod, the teacher from Room 8, would start to play the piano. That was the signal for Monica and the snow fairies to dance out. When they finished their dance, bells would jingle, and all the snow fairies were supposed to hide behind the trees. Then out came the reindeer pulling Santa on his sleigh, and Santa made a speech.

We practised it over and over. Every time I whooshed the loudest and waved the most. Nobody noticed.

Bobby Devlin kept going around saying "HoHoHo, be nice to me or you won't get any presents." Monica started tippy-toeing around and tapping everything with her magic wand. Even Lester melted whenever anybody was looking. They'll all watch me when I'm a star, I thought to myself.

As December 17 got closer and closer, nothing changed. I began to worry. Maggie was always busy with other things. She never had time to talk. I didn't even know if she had a plan yet. Maybe Maggie wasn't going to make me a star after all.

On dress rehearsal day, Room 7 was filled with spangles and stars and colours. Fantastic, I thought. I bet I'll be a big Christmas tree with lights and decorations.

When I saw my costume, I almost got sick. The trees had to wear brown shirts and brown sacks with arm holes and brown paper hats. We got brown paint on our faces and two branches to hold. They stuck bits of cotton all over us to look like snow.

No one noticed us at all. We might as well have been invisible.

"HO! HO! HO!" Bobby roared at me, "What do you want for Christmas, little boy?"

I didn't bother telling him.

Finally it was December 17, and I was pretty sure Maggie didn't have a plan. Afterwards she'll just pretend she forgot, I thought sadly.

After supper, I went to call for Maggie. As I scuffled my boots along the street, I imagined the bright stage and the dark hall full of people. All of them will wish they were in our play, I thought, because it's special.

Then I began to feel special too, because I *was* part of the show. I was the best tree in the whole forest, and that was where all the magic happened. I remembered that Christmas was coming too, and suddenly I wasn't sad at all. I raced the rest of the way to Maggie's. I couldn't wait to get started.

Maggie came out to meet me, and we headed down Greenapple Street to the school. Excitement hummed inside me. It felt strange to be going to school at night. Everything looked like I was seeing it for the first time. The fallen leaves crackled under our feet, and the street lights buzzed in the cold night air. It still hadn't snowed.

"Ever dark," I said. "There isn't one star."

"Just like the enchanted forest," Maggie said, "before I turn on the lights."

"If this were Hallowe'en, it would be spooky," I said. "But only good things happen at Christmas, even when it's dark, right?" Good things like your plan to make me a star, I thought, and waited for Maggie to tell me about it.

"That's right," said Maggie from behind me. Then she stuck her icy fingers down the back of my neck.

"Boo!" she yelled, and we ran the rest of the way to school.

We pulled open the doors and stepped into the light. People were buzzing around, doing a million things at once for our show. We hurried down the noisy hall to Room 7.

The classroom was crowded with elves and trees and reindeer and mice all getting on their costumes and makeup. Everybody talked at once.

"Hurry up, you two, and hang up your coats," called Mr. Flynn.

As Maggie turned to go to the gym, she said, "Remember, Cyril, be the best tree you can be, and you'll be a star."

"Sure," I said. I guessed that Maggie was trying to make me feel good. It was too late for a plan to work now, but she didn't want to say so. At least I wouldn't have to do her Christmas shopping.

I got on my costume, waved my branches a bit, and howled quietly. I did feel sort of like a tree. Maybe it was an okay costume after all. Then I went over to George and two of the elves.

"I saw him," said George. "He was talking to Mr. Flynn and writing stuff. And he had a bunch of cameras."

"Who?" I asked.

"The man from the newspaper. We're going to be in the paper."

"Wow," I said.

Lester walked by. His bottom half was in his snowman suit and his face was painted white.

"How many people will be here, Cyril?" he asked.

"Lots, I bet," I said. "And there's a man here to take pictures for the newspaper."

"What happens if you forget what to say?" Lester asked. "Bobby says everybody will boo and throw tomatoes, and a big hook will come out and pull you away."

"I don't think so," I said. "Besides, you're good. You won't forget."

"I think I might," Lester said. He looked very scared.

"Hey, Lester," yelled Bobby from across the room, "get ready for the hook. Gaaaack!" He pretended he was hooked.

"Cut it out, Bobby," said George. "Maybe you'll get the hook."

"No way," Bobby said. "I'm a star. I'm getting my picture taken for sure." Then he stole Monica's wand and wouldn't give it back until Mr. Flynn made him.

81

At almost 7:30, everyone gathered in our classroom. Mr. Flynn brushed up his moustache. It looked like there was going to be another announcement.

"Room 7," he said, "our play is about helping one another. I know that tonight all of you are going to help one another by trying the best you can. It doesn't matter whether you have a little to do or a lot. Everybody is important. If everybody helps, the people who came to watch us will enjoy our show. It can be our Christmas present to them."

We all got into line.

"You'd better help me," said Bobby in a loud voice. "Or I won't bring you any presents HoHoHo."

Monica almost whapped him with her magic wand, but Mr. Flynn said, "Ssshhhh!" We marched down the hall to the gym.

Backstage it was hot. Everybody bumped into everybody else and whispered back and forth. I slipped up to the curtain and peeked out.

The gym was filled with people talking and fussing with chairs and coats. My parents were out there somewhere.

Then I saw the newspaper reporter. He was holding one of his cameras and standing right by the stage. I thought again about being a star and having my picture in the paper. It wasn't going to happen now.

"Be the best tree you can be and leave the rest to me," whispered a voice in my ear. Then I saw Maggie hurrying over to run the lights. She's probably going to give me a tinfoil star or something, I thought.

"Places everyone," called Mr. Flynn.

I followed the other trees offstage. Maggie turned the light switches, and the gym went dark. The curtain pullers got ready. George and the choir fiddled with their clothes and hair. Then we all held our breath because our play was about to begin.

Slowly, Maggie changed the lights. The edges of the curtain got very bright as lights shone at the stage.

"Now," said Mr. Flynn.

He held the curtain open just a little, and George and the choir filed out. Then he closed it again. We all waited. It was quiet for a long time.

At last, George said, "Ladies and gentlemen: Welcome to Room 7's Christmas Assembly. Tonight...wewilltellyouthestoryofaChristmas-thatalmostdidn'thappen.Ourstorybeginswitha-song." Then he clumped over to the side of the stage really fast as people clapped. Being narrator seemed very scary to me all of a sudden. Bobby yawned.

Ms. Elrod sounded the piano, the choir hummed, and the song began. Everyone tried really hard. Some kids got lost part way through, but they almost got caught up by the end. There was lots more clapping. Bobby pinched his nose with one hand made a thumbs down sign with the other.

"PU," he said.

The choir slipped back inside the curtain, and the elves got ready on stage.

Out front, George said, "It's Christmas Eve at the North Pole, and the weather is stormy."

Maggie flipped more light switches. The curtain pullers heaved, and the elves started to work in Santa's shop. Bobby Devlin plumped up his stomach pillow and walked onstage.

Bobby gave a little wave to the audience and said, "HoHoHo." Then he made his speech about how he had to go out in spite of the bad weather because it wouldn't be Christmas if he didn't visit all the girls and boys.

What a joke, I thought. If Bobby Devlin were really Santa, he'd probably keep everything for himself, and stay home, and watch TV. But in the play, he and all the elves picked up sacks of presents to load on the sleigh and began to walk offstage as the curtains closed.

One of the elves tripped and bumped the others. Some presents went flying. The audience laughed, and a camera flash went off. The newspaper, I thought.

"Way to blow it," Bobby snapped backstage. Mr. Flynn sent him over to stand by Maggie.

I stood in a corner and watched as they changed the stage to make it look like the inside of a house. The family stood by the Christmas tree, and the mice got ready to scamper on as soon as the family went to bed.

Then I noticed something strange was happening at the light switches. Maggie was whispering to Bobby and nodding at the stage door. Bobby waited until Mr. Flynn wasn't looking and then hurried out. After he was gone, Maggie closed the stage door softly and stood in front of it. Her hands were behind her back, but I could tell they were moving. Then she went back to the lights.

When the mice finished their part, it was our turn. The trees hurried on and lifted their branches. My heart began to thump, thump, thump. It was time to be the best tree I could be, and this was a lot scarier than playing the piano ever was.

All the lights went out. We started to moan like the north wind, then the lights got brighter in our eyes. The piano started, and Monica and the fairies danced out and around the stage. Monica waved her magic wand, and at just the right moment the bells jingled. The music stopped, and all the fairies scurried to hide behind the trees. It was perfect.

Out pranced the reindeer. Everyone laughed. The sleigh slid out just right, and everyone laughed again. By now the stage was pretty crowded and the lights were pretty bright. It took a minute or so before anybody noticed that something was wrong. But then the reindeer stopped prancing, and the bells stopped jingling, and everyone got ready for Santa to say, "Bless my boots and bells, I can't be late!"

Nothing happened. We waited and waited, and no one said a thing. It got quieter and quieter in the gym. When was Santa going to make his speech? Then we looked at the sleigh and gasped. There was no Santa.

Nobody moved. I was almost too scared to breathe. Where was Bobby Devlin? The silence grew longer, and still nobody moved. The audience began to murmur. People were whispering backstage too, but I was too scared to look. Onstage, the lights were getting very hot.

Then I heard a rustling behind the curtain. A muffled voice said, "Now's your chance, Cyril." A foot pushed my rear end, and I barged out into the middle of the stage.

I didn't go alone. The branches were tangled up, so all the trees had to come with me. The fairies didn't want to be left out, so they scurried up behind us. I didn't want to be up front with everybody staring at me. This wasn't my idea. I started to shuffle backwards, dragging the other trees. The fairies leaped out of the way.

The foot pushed me out again.

This time the reindeer got their antlers stuck in

the tree branches, and they were pulled back too. The fairies leaped again, which gave Ms. Elrod the wrong idea about what was going on. She started to play the fairy dance all over again.

The fairies began dancing, and I kept sweeping around the stage. By now there were so many people all pushing and pulling that I couldn't stop. As we whirled, the lights began to flicker in time to the music. Everything swirled together until I didn't know what was what.

A thumping noise came from somewhere and then there was another sound—the audience was clapping along with the music. They were smiling and laughing. They thought we were all dancing. I was just trying to stop. Once more, waved Ms. Elrod and around we went again. At last we all slowed down and stopped.

The clapping was like a waterfall. I was so scared and dizzy that I didn't know what was happening. Then Monica tugged on my arm and told me to look at Ms. Elrod.

"Bow!" Ms. Elrod was saying, and she was looking at me.

I bent forward and bowed. I was still tangled up, so a lot of other people bowed with me. As I stood up straight, a camera flashed right in my eyes. When the stars cleared away, I saw the man from the newspaper in front of the stage. Everybody clapped all over again.

As the clapping died away, I heard the thumping sound again. It was coming from offstage, and it sounded a lot like somebody pounding on a door.

"Open this door!" came a voice. "You can't lock me out, I'm a star!"

"Someone opened the door, and Bobby Devlin came barrelling onto the stage.

"Where's the guy to take my..." he yelled, then stopped as he saw everybody staring at him.

"Bless my boots and bells!" he sputtered. "I can't be late!" The camera flashed again, the audience roared, and our play was back on.

The rest of the play was better somehow. We all knew that, even if somebody made a mistake, it would be okay. We would all help out.

That made it fun, and everybody had a good time, even Bobby Devlin. The audience thought his yelling was all part of the play, and they laughed and clapped for him at the end. He even started to act as though it was his own idea.

People clapped for me too, and for the other trees and the fairies and reindeer. I was a star after all. We were all stars after all.

Mr. Flynn never asked what happened. Maybe he didn't want to know since everything had worked out in the end.

All he said to me was, "Way to go, Cyril. I knew you'd do your best."

When it was time to go home, I waited with

Maggie by the front doors. Our parents were still talking to Mr. Flynn.

"What did you say to Bobby?" I asked.

"I told him a little lie," said Maggie. "I said the newspaper man wanted to take a picture of the star right away for tomorrow's paper. I told Bobby he'd meet him in Room 7. Bobby would do anything to get his picture in the paper, so I knew he'd wait around too long. Just to make sure, I locked the door as soon as he went out."

"Won't Bobby suspect?" I said.

"Maybe, but he'll look pretty dumb if he tells everybody how I tricked him. Anyway, he's happy now. And you're a star."

"Thanks for making me one," I said.

"No problem," said Maggie. She reached into her pocket and pulled out a shopping list five pages long.

I was too happy to care.

"Look," I said and pointed outside.

It was snowing.